Superphonics **Storybooks will he[lp]
learn to read using Ruth Miskin**[...] **effective
phonic method. Each story is fun to read and has
been carefully written to include particular sounds
and spellings.**

**The Storybooks are graded so your child can
progress with confidence from easy words to harder
ones. There are four levels - Blue (the easiest), Green,
Purple and Turquoise (the hardest). Each level is
linked to one of the core *Superphonics*® Books.**

ISBN: 978 0 340 80551 0

Text copyright © 2001 Gill Munton
Illustrations copyright © 2001 Jacqueline East

Editorial by Gill Munton
Design by Sarah Borny

The rights of Gill Munton and Jacqueline East to be identified as the
author and illustrator of this Work have been asserted by them
in accordance with the Copyright, Designs and Patents Act 1988.

First published in Great Britain 2001

10 9 8 7 6 5 4 3

All rights reserved. Apart from any use permitted under UK copyright
law, this publication may only be reproduced, stored or transmitted,
any form, or by any means with prior permission in writing of the
publishers or in the case of reprographic production in accordance with
the terms of licences issued by the Copyright Licensing Agency.

First published in 2001 by Hodder Children's Books,
a division of Hachette Children's Books,
338 Euston Road, London NW1 3BH
An Hachette UK Company. www.hachette.co.uk

Printed and bound in China by WKT Company Ltd.

A CIP record is registered by and held at the British Library.

Target words

This Turquoise Storybook focuses on the following sounds:

ir as in **bird** | **er** as in **fern**

ur as in **purse**

These target words are featured in the book:

bird's	dinner	properly
birthdays	faster	remember
dirty	fern	Rover
fir	flower	silver
first	Growler	slippers
girl's	her	superb
shirts	herbs	swerve
skirts	higher	terrier
third	interesting	tiger
thirteen	nerve	together
twirly	never	under
whirly	number	
	over	blur
creeper	perhaps	burglar
deserved	person	burgling

burn	furry	slurp
burp	further	surprise
burst	purple	turkey
curl	purr	turn
curtains	purse	
curve	Saturday	

(Words containing sounds and spellings practised in the Blue, Green and Purple Storybooks and the other Turquoise Storybooks have been used in the story, too.)

Other words

Also included are some common words (e.g. **there**, **where**) which your child will be learning in his or her first few years at school.

A few other words have been included, to help the story to flow.

Reading the book

1 Make sure you and your child are sitting in a quiet, comfortable place.

2 Tell him or her a little about the story, without giving too much away:

Growler is proud of being a cat burglar - but he changes his mind when he meets someone who is just as fast on his feet!

This will give your child a mental picture; having a context for a story makes it easier to read the words.

3 Read the target words (above) together. This will mean that you can both enjoy the story without having to spend too much time working out the words. Help your child to sound out each word (e.g. **f-ir-s-t**) before saying the whole word.

4 Let your child read the story aloud. Help him or her with any difficult words and discuss the story as you go along. Stop now and again to ask your child to predict what will happen next. This will help you to see whether he or she has understood what has happened so far.

Above all, enjoy the story, and praise your child's reading!

Cat Burglar

by Gill Munton

Illustrated by Jacqueline East

Hodder
Children's
Books

a division of Hachette Children's Books

I'm Growler.

I'm a cat burglar!

You should see me at work.
I can run faster than
the fastest cheetah!

I can climb higher than
the highest bird's nest!

I'm as BRAVE

as a TIGER!

Let's go cat burgling together.

It's Saturday night, and they're all out.

They never remember to lock their doors,

or shut their windows properly.

And that's where I come in!

Off we go!

We'll try this one first.

Under the fence ...

... over the rabbit hutch ...

... under the slide ...

... over the shed ...

... up the fir tree ...

... over the windowsill ...

... down the curtains ...

... and

IN!

Let's have a look in here.

Hmmm!

A girl's room!

Skirts ...

... shirts ...

... purple furry slippers (urgh!) ...

... Aha!

Here's her purse!

That's more like it!

Now for the getaway!

Up the curtains ...

... over the windowsill
(don't drop the purse)...

... down the fir tree ...

... over the shed ...

... under the slide ...

... over the rabbit hutch ...

... and under the fence.

OUT!!

See what I mean?

When I run, I'm just a blur!

A twirly, whirly, furry blur!

NO ONE can catch me!

I'm the best cat burglar in the world!

Off I go again!

Over the hedge ...

... over the car ...

... over the flower bed ...

... in the catflap

(very thoughtful!) ...

... round the kitchen ...

... up the stairs ...

... through the door ...

... and

IN!

Well, curl my claws!

What a messy person!

Shirts ...

... dirty socks (phwurr!) ...

... herbs ...

... a fern ...

... Aha!

Silver cuff links!

They'll look good on me!

Now for the getaway!

Through the door ...

... down the stairs ...

... round the kitchen ...

... out the catflap
(don't drop the
cuff links) ...

... over the flower bed ...

... over the car ...

... and over the hedge.

OUT!!

See what I mean?

When I climb, I'm just a blur!

A twirly, whirly, furry blur!

NO ONE can catch me!

I'm the best cat burglar in the world!

Off I go again!

Third time lucky!

And it's number thirteen –

my lucky number!

Up the creeper ...

... over the windowsill ...

... under the blind ...

... and IN!

Hmmm!

This IS interesting!

Turkey!

What a superb dinner!

All my birthdays have come together!

Slurp!

Slurp!

Burp!

Purrrr! Purrrr!

If I eat any more, I'll burst!

Hang on!

What's that?

Oh, no!

My worst nightmare!

A bull terrier –

And I'VE eaten his dinner!

Grrrr! Grrrr!

Grrrr! GRRR!

OK, don't panic!

Under the blind ...

... over the windowsill ...

... down the creeper
(I've dropped the purse!) ...

... swerve round the curve ...

... burn round the turn
(I've dropped the cuff links!) ...

... gasp - I can't run any further ...

... and HOME!

That was a nasty surprise!

Number thirteen wasn't lucky today!

But perhaps I deserved it.

Do you know, I think I've lost my nerve ...

I'm Growler.

I USED to be a cat burglar.

But now ...

... I'm just ...

... a cat!

Purrrr! Purrrr!